On the Mayflower

Voyage of the Ship's Apprentice & a Passenger Girl

by KATE WATERS

Photographs by
RUSS KENDALL

SCHOLASTIC PRESS
New York

Many thanks to the staff and volunteers at Plimoth Plantation, particularly: Liz Lodge, Vice-President, Museum Operations; Peter Arenstam, Manager, Maritime Artisans; John Reed, Bosun; Maureen Richards, Curator, Reproduction Collections; Doug Ozelius, Assistant Site Supervisor, *Mayflower II*; Jill Hall, Manager, Wardrobe Department; Joanna Kline, Deb Brewster, Ruth Hulse, and Kathi Bolt, Tailors; Tom Gerhardt, Artisan; Kathleen Curtin, Foodways Manager; and Carolyn Freeman Travers, Director of Research.

Many, many thanks to the young people in this book, and to their families: Mike Robbins, who plays William Small, and his parents Rick and Regina; Hila Bernstein, who plays Ellen Moore, and her parents Helen and Bruce; Hannah and Abigail Arenstam, and their parents Susan and Peter; Maeve Hannon, and her parents Moira and Jack; and Devin Orlander, and his parents Charlene and Todd.

And to the following staff and volunteers: Ted Curtin (Master Jones); Scott Mahon (Carpenter); David Goglia (Cook); Bill Ham (Passenger man); Matt Nisenoff (Gunner); Effie Mahon (Mrs. Hopkins); and Scott Atwood, Neil Beck, Stuart Bolton, Matt Cadorette, Michael Caliri, John Dever, Paul DiSalvatore, Steve Ewald, Will Gates, Joshua Gedraitis, Jim Gilrein, Chris Hall, Michael Hall, Fred Lonke, Angus McCamy, Justin McGonigle, Len Marsden, Jennifer Mooney, Bil Orland, Donald Severy, Marcus Sherman, Gene Trainor, Jonathan Trask, Peter Tufts, Keith White, and Pret Woodburn.

Additional thanks to: Billy Haverstock, David Walbridge, Jon Lane, Katherine A. Freeman, Anne Lane, George Cushman, and Priya Nair.

Photographer's assistants and additional photography by: Mark Dolan, Joe Gassner, Kris Kirby, and Thérèse Landry.

Ship diagram by Heather Saunders.

To Sarah, Emma, Christopher, and Nicholas Waters
and to Lucy, Heidi, and Patrick Waters Caldwell.
May fair winds carry you toward your dreams.
— K.W.

To my dearest friends Geoff and Andrea Rogers
and especially to their son, Angus William Rogers
— R.K.

Library of Congress Cataloging-in-Publication Data

Waters, Kate. On the *Mayflower:* voyage of the ship's apprentice and a passenger girl / by Kate Waters ; photographed by Russ Kendall.
p. cm.
Summary: A twelve-year-old apprentice and an eight-year-old passenger experience the first voyage of the *Mayflower.*
ISBN 0-590-67308-4
1. Pilgrims (New Plymouth Colony) — Juvenile fiction. [1. Mayflower (Ship) — Fiction. 2. Pilgrims (New Plymouth Colony) — Fiction.
3. Massachusetts — History — New Plymouth, 1620–1691 — Fiction.]
I. Kendall, Russ, ill. II. Title. PZ7.W26434 October 1996 [Fic] — dc20 95-43980 CIP AC

12 11 10 9 8 7 6 5 4 3 2   9/9 0 1/0

Printed in Mexico   49

First edition, October 1996

The display type was set in Ovidius Demi from Thaddius Szumilas
The text type was set in Stempel Schneidler by WLCR New York
Production supervision by Angela Biola
Design by Marijka Kostiw
The photographs in this book were taken with a Nikon F4 camera on 18mm, 55mm, 85mm, and 180mm Nikkor lenses.
Mr. Kendall used Fujichrome 100 and 400 film.

Prologue

On September 6, 1620, the ship Mayflower left England and sailed into the open Atlantic Ocean. The ship's destination was the northern parts of Virginia, near the mouth of the Hudson River. On board were the ship's master, Christopher Jones, about 30 officers and sailors, 102 passengers, and the ship's apprentice, William Small. Only two people on board had ever seen the land they were sailing to.

By God's grace.

My name is William Small, but I am called Will.

I am apprentice to Christopher Jones, master of the ship *Mayflower*.

I am learning to read maps and charts, to find our ship's position by the sun and stars, and to know the weather.

This is my second voyage.

I have never before been across the sea.

Truth be told, I am fair excited and a bit afraid.

"All hands predy to set sail."

"Courses in their gear."

As we leave Plymouth Harbor in England, I watch the sailors unfurl and set the sails.
The bosun calls out the orders.

"Heave on the mizzen halyard."

"Stand by to loose the forecourse sheets."

I am not yet tall enough to climb the rigging, so
I help belay the lines.
   The lines are awkward and sticky with tar.

I look back at the land and think of my family.
I wonder when I will see them again.

Once at sea, Master Jones teaches me to measure the position of the sun and the horizon with a quadrant.

It is hard to hold the quadrant steady as the ship pitches and rolls on the waves.

My knees will ache mightily until I get accustomed to the motion again!

In the Round House, we compare the readings to the charts, and Master Jones sets our course for North America.

At night, when the winds die down, the motion settles somewhat.

Now I hear the passengers in the 'tween decks.

They sing and pray with good voice!

I can smell their food and hear their children squeal and run about.

When I fetch the Master's meal of oatmeal and peas and pork, John Reynolds, the cook, grumbles about the praying and the chatter.

I serve Master Jones; John Clarke, the pilot; and William Hall, the bosun.

They are in good spirits now that we are under sail.

After our meal, John Clarke begins my lessons on the traverse board, which we use to mark the ship's direction and speed.

On my way to my bed, I peek down through the hatch.

The Master would not like me spying, but the people below are a curiosity to me.

'Tis a small space for 102 people and their belongings.

I can hear the passengers complaining about the close quarters and the pitching of the ship.

I am grateful to be up here where there is room to walk about.

The days continue fair and the passengers seem used to being at sea.

First thing of a morning, I haul seawater to wet the boards to keep them tight.

A passenger girl comes on deck to empty a chamber pot.

Though I should not linger, I am bold to address her.

She says she is called Ellen Moore and is traveling without her parents.

"How do you keep your days below?" I ask.

"'Tis mostly tiresome," she answers. "There is so little space and so many people. But I am kept busy."

"I pit prunes to help with the cooking."

"I mend garments."

"I pass the time playing."

"I wet cloths for those with seasickness . . ."

"...and I wonder about this place, North America."

We have prosperous winds, and Ellen and I converse often.

Then, over half the seas crossed, the winds begin to blow mightily and it gets fearsome cold.

One morning, I hear the Master's whistle summoning me to the Round House.

"A storm is coming, younker," he shouts. "Be quick."

"'Tis likely to be rough since it is autumn. We must mark our course well."

He gives everyone their orders.

The sailors clew up and furl the sails against approaching wind.

There will be no steering the ship during the storm.

We will drift in the hands of God.

I call for Ellen and give her the Master's orders.

"Douse your cooking fire and all lanterns. A single spark could set the ship afire. Secure all that is likely to roll about. The hatch will be covered until the waves calm. Be brave."

When night falls, the winds blow more fiercely.
The sea roars enough to make me deaf.
The waves throw water everywhere.

Shivering in my hammock, I hear the sailors running to and fro and the mates shouting orders above the wind.

I think of the passengers below in the darkness and cold.

No one will have time for their concerns until the danger to the ship is past.

There are days and nights of fearful dark, and wind, and rain.

I am kept more busy than before.

I help the gunner relash the cannon that has loosened during the night.

I pour drink for the tired sailors and listen to their talk.

Some fear the ship is not sufficient to withstand the storm.

One day, when the storm seems less hard, I uncover the hatch and call Ellen.

She comes on deck and gulps the cold, damp air. "You are fortunate to be up here in the wind," she tells me. "'Tis so close and rank below, and 'tis cruel with only cold food. Everyone suffers from seasickness, and I am kept busy tending them. I worry so for Mrs. Hopkins, who is large with child and cannot find a way to rest."

The storm does not relent.
One howling day, the carpenter rouses me.
"Quick, lad, we've leaks to fix. Every man must help."
My stomach drops at this dire news.

I carry the carpenter's caulking mallets, irons, and the oakum, and climb down into the hold.

Black, rank water wets my shoes.
We caulk the leaks and more open up.
It seems to take hours upon hours.
It is hard to hammer true with the ship rocking as she is.

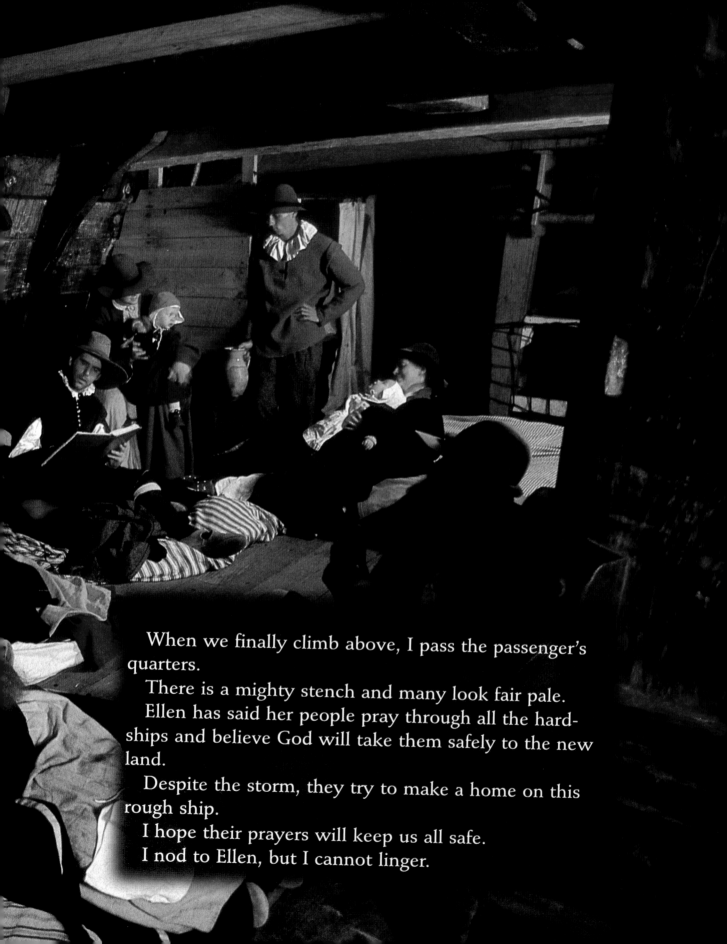

When we finally climb above, I pass the passenger's quarters.

There is a mighty stench and many look fair pale.

Ellen has said her people pray through all the hardships and believe God will take them safely to the new land.

Despite the storm, they try to make a home on this rough ship.

I hope their prayers will keep us all safe.

I nod to Ellen, but I cannot linger.

In a fortnight the skies begin to clear. On my way across the deck, I see the hatch open a bit.

Ellen peeks out, and starts when she sees me.

"Will," she whispers, "is it over? Are we safe? Mrs. Hopkins had her baby three days ago! I don't think we can bear any more!"

"'Twill be calm now, pray God," I answer. "The Master will give you leave to be on deck as soon as he is sure."

When the passengers come up to get air, Mrs. Hopkins shows me her baby. He is named Oceanus, after the sea.

What a tiny creature to ride out such a storm!

I mend a sail while Ellen tells the news.

I tell her about the fearsome days and nights of the storm and the constant tasks and errands I had to do.

"'Twas just as bad below," she says. "Some said they'd lief die than suffer through one more day of such rocking. But our prayers were answered."

Then, on that day, we hear gulls.
Gulls mean land is near!

But by our bearings, we are bound for the land called Cape Cod, not Virginia where the passengers have a patent to settle.

The storm has taken us off our course.

After a day of trying to sail south past the perilous shoals of Cape Cod, the Master meets with the passengers. They agree to try to find safe harbor there since winter is upon us.

The next day, I see leaves and branches floating in the water. It has been 65 days since we departed from England.

Suddenly, there is a cry from the working tops.

"LAND HO!"

We anchor in a protected harbor, and the passengers
set about exploring the land.

During the months that the passengers build their
houses in this cold place, the ship is still their home.

Ellen is given leave to come on deck more often, and
I have fewer chores to do.

We teach each other songs and tell stories of our lives
at home.

But mostly we talk about the hardship of the voyage.

"I can survive anything, now," Ellen tells me.

"Indeed, you are brave," I tell her.

With their houses built, the last passengers leave the ship.

As the *Mayflower* sets sail for England, I feel sad, for I will miss Ellen. She has been my family in these days.

Looking back on the land, I can see the roofs of dwellings and the smoke from cooking fires.

I wonder if I shall see Ellen again.

May God grant you well in this new land, my friend.

More About the *Mayflower*

The *Mayflower*

The *Mayflower* was a typical 17th-century, three-masted merchant ship. Until this voyage in 1620, she had traveled from England to France, Norway, and Germany, trading English cloth for wine, spices, and fish. This was her first voyage across the Atlantic Ocean to North America and her first voyage carrying people instead of cargo.

The *Mayflower* was brightly painted. (Seamen could identify ships by their colors.) A hawthorn flower, which is also called the mayflower in England, may have been carved on her stern. She may have flown pennants as well as a flag of the cross of Saint George, a red cross on a white background. Saint George is the patron saint of England.

Ships like the *Mayflower* were designed to sail before the wind. By adjusting the sails and moving the whipstaff to move the rudder, the pilot navigated, or conned, the ship. There were 55 live, or working, lines on the *Mayflower* used to adjust the sails. All the sailors were kept very busy. In a storm, sails were clewed up and then furled so that they would not hold wind, and the ship was allowed to drift.

The *Mayflower II*

The photographs in this book were taken on the *Mayflower II*. She is a reproduction of what historians think the original *Mayflower* looked like. She was built in England to honor the close links between England and the United States. The modern-day builders who built the *Mayflower II* used only methods that shipbuilders would have used in the 17th century. They built her by hand, and it took almost two years. The *Mayflower II* set sail from Plymouth, England, on April 20, 1957, and arrived in Plymouth Harbor, Massachusetts, on June 13, 1957. She is now one of four museum exhibits at Plimoth Plantation in Plymouth, Massachusetts. The other three are the 1627 Pilgrim Village, Hobbamock's (Wampanoag Indian) Homesite, and the Carriage House Crafts Center. Each is a living history exhibit where you can see and experience how people of the 17th century lived. In the Village, actors, called interpreters, play the parts of actual people of that time. At the Homesite, the staff speaks from the 20th-century perspective. If you visit the *Mayflower II*, you will see for yourself how tiny the ship was that carried so many people's hopes and dreams to this shore.

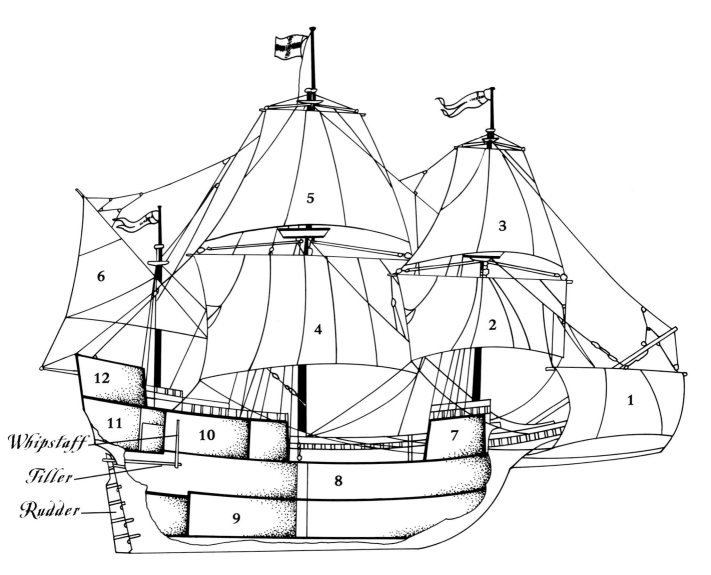

Diagram of the Mayflower with her sails and important areas labeled.

Labels on diagram: Whipstaff, Tiller, Rudder

1. SPRITSAIL

2. FORECOURSE

3. FORE-TOPSAIL

4. MAIN COURSE

5. MAIN-TOPSAIL

6. MIZZEN SAIL

7. FO'C'SLE
   This is where meals were cooked for the crew.

8. 'TWEEN DECKS
   This is where the passengers lived during the journey.

9. HOLD
   This is where food, drink, tools, and supplies were stored.

10. STEERAGE
    This is where the helmsman steered the ship by moving the whipstaff, the long lever that moves the tiller, which moves the rudder. An officer on the deck above steerage gave the orders.

11. GREAT CABIN
    This is where the ship's master, some of the officers, and the ship's apprentice slept.

12. ROUND HOUSE
    This is the chartroom from which the master directed the ship's course.

The 1620 Voyage of the *Mayflower*

There are only two first-person accounts of the famous 1620 voyage of the *Mayflower* to North America. Both are by passengers. Each is only a few pages and gives very little detail about day-to-day life on the ship. Additional information about the voyage has been gathered from accounts of other voyages telling what this kind of trip was like and also from what we know about navigating and shipboard life in the 17th century.

The *Mayflower* left England much later than its master and passengers had hoped to leave. First, there were disagreements with the people who had loaned the passengers the money to hire two ships. Then, one of the ships, the *Speedwell*, had to turn back because it was leaking badly. Finally, with most of the passengers from the *Speedwell* crowded onto the *Mayflower*, the voyage began.

Because they were late leaving, they encountered autumn storms on the Atlantic Ocean that were particularly severe.

By the time the ship came into Plymouth Harbor, it was winter. The crew and passengers had not had fresh food in several weeks. The cold and damp, along with their poor nutrition, caused many people to get sick. Between November 9, 1620, when land was sighted, and April 5, 1621, when the *Mayflower* finally left to return to England, half the passengers and half the crew had died.

The *Mayflower* stayed in Plymouth for five months not only to tend to the sick but also so that the passengers would have someplace to live while they built their houses and prepared their gardens. That is not work people usually do in the winter, so it took a long time. And unfortunately, the thatched roof of the first house they built was destroyed by fire.

Finally, as spring was coming, Master Jones determined that the passengers were able to be self-sufficient, and he turned the *Mayflower* back toward England.

Who Was Christopher Jones?

Christopher Jones was the master of the *Mayflower*. He was responsible for the smooth running of the ship, her safety, and the safety of her passengers. He was a quarter-owner of the *Mayflower* and therefore shared in her profits. It is likely that he had an apprentice on board, although no apprentice's name appears in the records of the voyage.

Who Was William Small?

William Small is an invented character, but the facts about his life were common to young ship's apprentices of the time. A smart young boy would have been apprenticed to a ship's master for seven years. He would have had to have been good in mathematics and to have had a sharp eye and a love of the sea. His job was to learn the craft of a mariner and all the navigation skills needed to sail a ship. He might have hoped to be a mate one day, or even a master.

Who Was Ellen Moore?

Ellen Moore was eight years old when she traveled to North America on the *Mayflower* in 1620. Because of a family tragedy, she and her sister and two brothers were sent on the journey with other families. Ellen was assigned to Edward Winslow's family.

There is no information about Ellen in the records of Plymouth Colony. It is likely that she succumbed to the sickness that killed half the passengers and half the crew while the ship lay in Plymouth Harbor during the winter of 1620–1621.

Who Is Mike Robbins?

Mike Robbins plays the part of William Small in this book. He was thirteen years old when the photographs were taken. Mike has been a volunteer on the *Mayflower II* since he was nine. He works with his dad, who restores old ships.

Mike has an older brother and sister. He likes water skiing and snow skiing as well as sailing. During the summer, he does volunteer work at a science day camp in Massachusetts. He hopes to stay involved with Plimoth Plantation and the *Mayflower II*.

Mike dreams of playing hockey for the Boston Bruins when he is older and trains hard to reach his goal.

About the photo shoot, Mike says that the highlight was being able to sail on the *Mayflower II* and meeting a lot of new people.

Who Is Hila Bernstein?

Hila Bernstein plays the part of Ellen Moore in this book. She was ten years old when the photographs were taken. When Hila read *Sarah Morton's Day: A Day in the Life of a Pilgrim Girl,* she knew she wanted to become an interpreter. Her dream was realized, and she has been volunteering at Plimoth Plantation since she was eight. Her favorite activities in the Village include milking the goats, plucking ducks, and cooking village foods.

In school, Hila enjoys writing and math, but her favorite activity and subject is reading. She plays soccer and basketball in her free time and studies violin and keyboard.

Hila would like to be an actress and a playwright, but if that doesn't work out, she would like to be an archaeologist or anthropologist.

The photo shoot taught Hila that one has to practice, practice, and practice in order to get the best result. She says that the group passenger photo was the hardest because she had to be so still while Russ shot many rolls of film.

Glossary